Hanna, Homeschooler

By Suki Wessling

Illustrated by Megan Trever Ryan

CHATOYANT

Chatoyant
PO Box 832
Aptos, CA 95001
www.Chatoyant.com

Publisher's Cataloging in Publication Data
Wessling, Suki.
Hanna, Homeschooler / Suki Wessling.
    p. cm.
Summary: Living in a new town, young homeschooler
Hanna struggles to adjust to her new home and make friends.
ISBN 978-0-9661452-7-4
[1. Schools—Juvenile Fiction. 2. Kindergarten—Juvenile
Fiction.]
Printed in the United States.
Library of Congress Control Number: 2015915000

For Charlotte,

my original homeschooler

Chapter 1

Hanna sat in the window seat looking out at the grey morning. It was seven-thirty, and usually she wouldn't be dressed yet. But she dressed for this morning.

The two girls across the street, first Kira and then Cassie, came out of their houses. They were right on time.

Kira and Cassie were going to the first day of school. Hanna wasn't. She sat in the window seat, thinking about that.

Hanna had only moved into this house during the summer. A few months before, her dad had lost his job. Mom said Gram needed help with the big house now that Gramp was gone. So they moved from their cabin in the Sierra mountains to Central California, where Mom had grown up.

It was flat, and hot, and there were so many

houses. They had left behind Hanna's friend, Henry, and all the trees that Hanna knew like people.

Hanna's dad had been leaving home early to go to school. He was training to be a nurse, which Kira said was weird. Mom explained that being a nurse was a good job, but in the past, only women did it.

But Dad was doing it because he wanted to help people. Hanna didn't think that was weird.

Kira and Cassie were different than any kids Hanna had known. Hanna wondered if they thought she was weird, too.

Kira and Cassie's moms backed their cars into the street and were gone.

"What are you doing up so early, pumpkin?" Mom asked Hanna, coming up behind and kissing her head.

Hanna squirmed away.

"Uh-oh, the rare spiny pumpkin has come to our house again!" Mom said. "What do you see happening out there on those manicured lawns?"

"Kira and Cassie went to school," Hanna said. "I wonder what they are going to do for the first day. What are we going to do today?"

"Oh, I don't know," Mom said, stroking Hanna's

hair. "I'd like to do some baking."

Hanna sighed. That didn't sound like much of a plan.

Hanna's mom was very busy with the baby, David, who was really not a baby anymore. He was born early and spent months inside an incubator getting big enough to come home, so Mom said he'd be like a baby a little longer than other kids.

David was almost two and he crawled almost as fast as Hanna could walk. Hanna's mom said Gram's house was a babyproofing nightmare. Gram fought with Mom about moving her knickknacks up out of the kids' reach. Gram said her house was looking all disarranged.

When she thought Hanna wasn't listening, Mom

told Dad the house was like a dusty *tschatschke* shop. That word was pronounced "chach-kah." That was Mom's word for all Gram's stuff. Gram didn't like to get rid of anything.

Hanna liked Gram's stuff—each thing had a story. And she liked the window seat where she could sit and see so much action.

Mom went off to dress David and Hanna wandered into Gram's room.

Gram used to sleep in the big master bedroom upstairs where Mom and Dad were sleeping now, but she wasn't so good with stairs now. Her room was back behind the living room and had wine-colored wallpaper with a flower pattern. Gram called it the "den," which made Hanna think it used to be inhabited by lions. But Mom told her it used to be the TV room.

Gram had a TV in there, and it was always on, playing the weather.

"Hi Gram," Hanna said from the doorway. Her parents had told her not to go in unless she was invited.

"Hannietta," Gram said. She was sitting at her vanity so her reflection looked at Hanna. "Come in."

Hanna sniffed as she entered the room. The whole house smelled like Gram, but it was strongest in this room. Dust, roses, and furniture polish.

Gram turned. She had a little object in her hand, which shook like she was cold. Hanna knew that Gram used to make beautiful things like the quilt on Hanna's bed. Now her hands wouldn't let her sew or knit anymore.

"You can help me with this, dear," she said.

Hanna stood over her and looked down at the yellowed book on Gram's vanity. It had pictures stuck on with little black corners, which was what Gram had in her hand. Hanna noticed that one corner was missing from around a photo of a smiling man in a uniform.

"It's so hard for me to place these, now," Gram said, letting Hanna take the corner from her hand. "Can you lick it and stick it on that corner?"

Hanna licked the back of the little corner and eased it onto the photo. She and Gram pressed down their fingers one on top of the other to stick it down.

"That's Gramps," she said to Hanna.

"Gramps?" Hanna was surprised. He was young and thin and had a full head of hair. The Gramps

Hanna remembered was old and thin and quiet.

"Haven't you seen my photos yet?" Gram answered. "Oh, I have so many. From when I was a child, when your grandfather and I married, when your mother was young."

Gram pointed to the handsome young Gramps and a group shot of young men in uniform. "This was when Gramps went to war. Did you know he was a fighter pilot?"

Hanna shook her head.

"Oh, yes, he was a hero!" Gram exclaimed. "He went overseas and shot down enemy planes. Then his plane was shot down and we didn't hear from him for two years."

Gram's face softened into that faraway look she got.

"His family and my family lived across the street from each other in Brooklyn, you know. In New York. We knew each other before we knew each other!"

Gram bubbled with laughter.

"We always knew each other's business because from our living room you could see right into his. I remember the day the telegram came saying he was missing in action—the army didn't know where he was, but they thought the Germans had probably caught him. That day I saw the telegraph boy go up the steps of his house and I ran across the street and was there before they'd even had a chance to read it. I can still hear his father reading that telegram, and his mother trying not to cry, and his little sister—that's Aunt Molly—saying, What does it mean? What does it mean?"

Hanna considered this story.

"So Aunt Molly was a little girl?" she asked doubtfully. Aunt Molly had always seemed even older and stricter than Gram.

Gram bubbled with laughter again. "Why, yes, dear, she was nearly ten years younger than George. Haven't you ever seen our family tree?"

"What's a family tree?" Hanna asked.

"Let's draw one!" a voice said cheerfully from the door. It was Mom, who'd been watching with David balanced on her hip. "Come on!"

Gram and Hanna followed Mom out of Gram's bedroom.

Mom opened the cabinet in the dining room which she'd emptied of Gram's stuff so she could keep homeschooling supplies. She drew out an enormous roll of white butcher paper, placed David on the floor, and rolled it out. She fixed the paper at each end of the long dining room table with tape and then ripped off the roll.

Meanwhile, Gram had figured out what Mom was up to. She'd taken out Hanna's bucket of markers. She wrote Rosa Weinstein in red at the top of the butcher paper and circled it. Next to that, she wrote Schmuel Schimmelfarb in blue. Gram's letters were shaky like the scary letters on Halloween posters.

"Can you help me, Hannietta?" Gram asked. "Under Rosa, write 1884, and under Schmuel, write 1878."

Hanna was surprised when lunchtime came. She and Gram had munched on apples and muffins while the family tree spread and grew down the paper so they had to connect some of the people with snaking long lines.

When she looked at it, Hanna did think it looked like a tree, with long, long roots. Gram could remember all the names and almost all the birthdates without looking at her book, but after they were done she got out her book and showed Hanna pictures of all these people who were related to Hanna. There were so many! And they came from countries in the world that didn't even exist anymore.

After lunch, Mom printed out a map of Europe and Hanna outlined and shaded in where Austria-Hungary was when Rosa and Schmuel had left and come to America by ship. The ship only had sails and no motor! Then Hanna went outside to swing and climb the tree, while Mom and Gram helped David learn how to use the baby slide.

"Are you really so set on keeping her out of school?" Hanna heard Gram ask. "Do you really think she'll learn what she needs to?"

Sometimes Gram and Mom talked grown-up talk that made Hanna feel like she was just a name on the family tree.

Later, when she was sure they were home, Hanna got permission to go across the street to see Kira and Cassie. She found them talking at Cassie's swingset, looking serious and proud.

"My teacher's name is Mrs. Conger," Cassie said. "We made our handprints with finger paint and traced our names under them to put on the wall."

Cassie, Hanna knew, was in kindergarten. She didn't know how to read yet, but she was big and strong and Hanna liked her funny laugh.

"My teacher's name is Mr. Greg," Kira said. "My mom was afraid I wouldn't like a boy teacher, but he's so nice. And in first grade, we don't have to take naps like kinders."

"What did you do in school today?" Kira asked Hanna.

Hanna felt their curious eyes on her as she felt her face get hot.

"Oh, nothing," she said. "We just baked muffins."

chapter 2

Hanna sat in the window seat looking out at the grey morning. It was eight o'clock, and she had watched Kira and Cassie get rushed into their cars again. Nothing else new had happened.

Mom came in, balancing David on her hip. David was chewing on an old stuffed cat Hanna hadn't seen since they moved.

"Momma!" Hanna screamed. "That's mine!"

Hanna grabbed the slimy package from David, who started to scream. She pounded up the stairs and into her room, which had been Mom's room. It was papered with rose wallpaper and had a four poster bed. It had three of Gram's old photos in proud, gold-painted picture frames on the wall. The dresser had actual scrolls carved into it.

But that didn't matter. Nothing mattered except that her cat was slimy and disgusting. Hanna threw herself on the bed, and then threw the cat across the room. She wasn't crying quite hard enough not to notice that it made a satisfying "splat" sound when it hit the wallpaper and slid down.

Hanna howled and cried and she wondered how long it was going to take Mom to get there. She was getting tired.

But Mom didn't seem to get the hint. Hanna stopped howling and turned over on her back to look at the stick-on stars Dad had put on the ceiling, just like on the ceiling of their cabin in the mountains.

"The stars are the same here," he said to her. He told her they'd be moving and leaving behind their cabin, her favorite tree with the hiding hole inside, and the stars on the ceiling of her little room.

"Not only that," Mom added. "You'll have your own room and the four-poster bed that was Gram's when she was a little girl. Then it was mine. Now it will be yours."

Hanna didn't think it was such a great trade-off. There was no hiding hole in any tree here, and when she woke in the middle of the night, the sky glowed from all the streetlights and stores.

Even worse, Hanna thought, there would be no

snow this year.

And worst of all, Hanna had no friend here like Henry, who always knew what she wanted to do.

Hanna was getting ready for another good cry when she heard Mom's voice at the doorway.

"I'm glad you stopped that howling," Mom said. "Dad got in late last night and he needs his sleep. Do you want to go for a walk?"

In the mountains, Mom and Hanna and David had gone for a walk every day, but Mom had been busy getting settled into their new home. Hanna sat up, interested.

"Where?" she asked. There didn't seem to be anywhere to walk here but on the grid of roads that just led to strip malls or the park.

Mom shrugged. "Wherever we find."

Mom walked over and grabbed Hanna in a big bear hug. It felt strange and new, even though it used to happen all the time.

"Where's David?" Hanna asked.

"Downstairs. Gram said she'd work on feeding him."

Mom got a funny grin on her face and Hanna had to giggle, too. David was the pickiest baby any-body ever met. When he didn't like something, he let you put a big spoonful of it into his mouth and then he'd blow it out so it splattered everywhere. Dad called him Hurricane David. Mom sighed. She knew she'd be down on her hands and knees finding creamed carrots all over Gram's clean baseboards.

"I wonder if the people living in our cabin have found all the rice cereal he spit into the woodstove yet," Hanna said.

"The mice likely found it before they did," Mom replied with a smile. "Come on, Hanna-bug. Let's get ready for a walk."

Hanna and Mom came out into the air that was already dry and stale like old crackers. Mom had David strapped on her back and she carried a big shoulder bag full of food. Hanna carried her backpack with her binoculars, her sketchbook, and colored pencils, plus Mom's old book, *Birds of California*. Hanna didn't believe they'd find any nature, and neither did Gram.

"It's so built up now," Gram said. "I do like having convenient shopping. Do you know, when Gramps and I moved here, we thought we were on the edge of nowhere!"

Mom reminded Gram that when she was a girl, there was a stream and foxes and coyotes living where there were houses now. "We'll see what we can find," Mom said.

"Where are we going to go?" Hanna asked Mom. They walked down the front walk to the street.

"I think we should try to take a walk down memory lane," Mom said.

"Where's that?" Hanna asked.

"That's a pretend place," Mom explained. "But it's also real. It's the place I grew up in. It's still here, but people put houses and roads on top of it. So we're going to have to act like detectives and try to find my memories."

"Are we going to have to lift up any houses?" Hanna asked. She'd seen people come in and buy cabins in their neighborhood in the mountains and lift them up on stilts to pour concrete underneath them. Mom laughed.

"I think we'd get arrested!" she said. She took Hanna's hand. "Let's see if we can find the stream first."

Mom told Hanna that when she was a girl, her house was one block away from where the houses just stopped and the wild land began. She and her friends would go out there and follow the stream, which only filled up during big rains, and look for lizards to catch and bunnies to chase.

"I figure the stream is in here somewhere," she told Hanna. "Remember how when we're going up to the park we have to go on that curvy road, Collier? Why would they make it curvy?"

Hanna thought a moment. "To make it fun like a roller coaster?"

Mom smiled.

"To make it pretty?"

Mom smiled.

"To write words you can read from airplanes?"

Mom laughed. "That's a good one," she said. "I think it might have something to do with the stream."

They walked the block up from Gram's house like they were going to the park, but they walked the other way on the curvy street, Collier. Mom peered between each house and mentioned that she could see native trees behind them.

Hanna didn't think that was unusual but Mom did. They went around another curve and Mom stopped in front of an overgrown path that went between two houses.

"Well, look at this," she said.

Hanna looked, raised her binoculars, and looked again. The plants formed a green and brown fuzz in her binoculars. Mom waited as if Hanna should say something.

"Look at what?" Hanna said.

"Where do you think this path goes?" Mom asked her.

Hanna had grown up in a place with paths all over. No one really had much that you would call a yard, not like here. You couldn't grow grass or even many bought flowers up in the mountains, so people's yards looked a lot like the woods: trees, the low-growing plants, and wildflowers in the early summer.

"In a place like this, a dirt path can only mean adventure!" Mom announced. She grabbed Hanna's hand and they turned off the sidewalk.

The path was not wide, but it was also clear that someone was using it. The soil underfoot was packed hard, so hard it wasn't even dusty. They walked past a white house, which had wooden fence around it. Peering through the fence, Hanna could see a green, green lawn and flowers in a square around a large hot tub.

"Come on," Mom whispered as if they were doing something very, very secret. "Look at this."

The trail went up and curved behind the back fence and then over a small rise. Mom sucked in her breath in wonder. Hanna stood and looked.

It was a dry streambed filled with concrete. Hanna could see tangles of plants on either side, and a line of people's back fences.

"This is it," Mom said in a whisper. "I used to come here every day. Of course, it wasn't concrete then."

She walked into the streambed and sat down on a largish rock that had rolled down there. Hanna crouched next to her, and David peered wide-eyed over Mom's shoulder.

"Listen," Mom said.

They sat for a very long time, and slowly, over the traffic noise and the hum of electricity and the sound of voices from someone's TV, Hanna heard what Mom was listening to.

Birds. A scratching sound. The whiz of an insect past her face. A cheeping kind of bird. The rustle of dry trees. A dusty, slow, late summer sound.

"This is where I grew up," Mom whispered. "My

world, it's still here. After all this time."

"Why is it paved?" Hanna asked.

"Oh, they do that so they don't have to deal with erosion. Streams have a way of going where they want to, you know."

"It doesn't seem nice to the stream," Hanna said.

Her mom smiled. "No, it doesn't. How about we go up the streambed and see if we can find where the concrete ends?"

They walked up the concrete like it was a strange sort of sunken sidewalk. On either side, it was the same: fence joining fence, weeds, scraggly trees, birds.

Mom stopped suddenly. "Oh, look!" she whispered.

Hanna saw a fat little lizard sunning himself in the middle of the streambed. His face snapped to attention when Mom pointed, and he sat very still, watching them. All of a sudden, faster than she could say a word, the lizard zipped into the brush.

They continued walking until the stream curved, and when they came to the other side of the curve, what they found was a surprise: a tall, cinderblock wall, with an enormous concrete pipe sticking out of it. The pipe was stained in the bottom as if by dirty water, but it was dry. It was big enough for Hanna to stand in.

"Can I climb in there?" Hanna asked. She felt like she should ask, though she'd never asked anything like that about a big boulder at home. This seemed different, dangerous.

"Of course," Mom said. "I'll just sit here."

Hanna noticed that David was asleep with his head on Mom's shoulder, drooling on her shirt. Mom lowered herself down carefully and set her bag in front of her.

Hanna climbed into the pipe and moved in a few feet. She could just see daylight at the other end if she crouched down. She noticed that the sound of her scuffing feet magnified and repeated up the pipe.

"Hoo!" she said.

"Ooh ooh ooh!" the echo repeated.

"Yow!" she called.

"Eow eow eow!" the echo repeated.

Hanna turned to look at Mom, who laughed. "An echo," Mom said. "Like in Miners' Canyon. Remember Dad yodeling there?"

"Yodel-ay-hee-hoo!" Hanna called out down the pipe.

"Odel-ay-ee odel-ay-ee!" the echo called back.

"It's not such a smart echo," Hanna said to her mom, climbing back out.

"Because of the shape of the tunnel," Mom explained. "The sound waves are changing shape as they get back to you."

Mom's hands formed waves out and back from her body as she pretended to make an echo. "Yoo! Ooh, ooh!"

Mom had set out containers of snacks she'd brought—crackers, cheese, and grapes. Hanna ate in silence, thinking about the tunnel and the lizard, listening to birds chirping and the whiz of insects.

Later that afternoon, Hanna sat on the swing in Cassie's yard, listening to Cassie and Kira talk. They knew a big girl who could do all the monkey bars, all the way across, and who called Cassie a "kinder-baby."

"What did you do in school today?" Cassie asked.

Hanna shrugged. "We went for a walk," she offered.

Kira and Cassie stared at her.

"Mom says you should go to school," Kira said

finally.

Hanna didn't know what to say. She looked at her hands.

"Hey," Kira said, "Let's see who can do the most monkey bars at my house!"

They all ran out of Cassie's fenced yard and in the gate to Kira's, where Kira, who could practice monkey bars any time she wanted, showed them that she could do five while they each could only do three.

Chapter 3

Hanna's mom heard about a homeschooling group that met in a park. It wasn't their park—this one was quite a long drive. Hanna's mom wondered if David would make it. David hadn't spent much time in cars yet, so he was bad at it. He didn't like his carseat. He screamed and wanted to nurse the second they got moving.

Hanna was curious about meeting other homeschoolers in their new town. If they had stayed in the mountains, she would have just been with the kids she knew, and they were homeschoolers, too, Hanna thought. No one there said it was weird. No one Hanna knew, anyway.

Hanna was also nervous. She wondered if the other homeschoolers did things like in school. Did they have a desk where they did seat work? Did they have a cubby and a pencil box and all the other things Kira and Cassie had told her about?

David fought and screamed when Mom put him into his carseat, but then he sat still because Mom gave him one of Gram's fancy spoons to suck on. Hanna sat next to him and read all the signs to him as they passed them.

"Keep in touch with Sprint," she read from a sign. "No left turn."

They stopped at a light.

"Es…" Hanna paused.

"Estates," Mom finished for her.

"Estates," Hanna read. "What does B-L-V-D mean?"

"Boulevard," Mom said. "That's supposed to be a street with trees down the middle. And estates are fancy houses."

"But Estate Boulevard doesn't have trees at all," Hanna pointed out. "It just has stores."

"I know," Mom said. "I think they named it that because it sounded fancy."

"Boulevard does sound fancy," Hanna said. "It sounds like that boulevard should be full of lard!"

Mom laughed. "Now, that's fancy," she said.

They got to the park and Mom drove all around three sides of it before she found a parking spot.

Just as she was concentrating on backing in, David threw his spoon into the front seat and started to scream.

"Boulevard, full of lard!" Hanna sang to him. "Pull a card, very hard!"

But David wasn't interested in Hanna's rhymes. Mom made soothing noises as she parked the car, then she said, "OK, Hannietta, you can get out while I soothe the screaming beast."

Hanna let Mom sit in her seat while she stood out on the grass. David quieted as soon as Mom lifted him from his seat.

Hanna saw that another mom was striding across the grassy area toward their car. Or Hanna thought she was a mom. She was very tall, and she wore a long, flowing colorful skirt, and her hair was wrapped up in a many-colored scarf.

"Molly!" the woman called out, waving her hand. Then she laughed and put her hands over her mouth like a little girl giggling. "Oh, I'm sorry. My friend drives that very same car and she has a girl just your size."

Mom poked her head out of the car. "Another mother West of the Rockies drives this car?" she asked. Mom didn't like Gram's big old car, which she called The Boat. It was a dark green car with wide black leather seats and, Mom said, an engine that roared like a jet.

"She inherited hers from her father," the woman said.

"This is my mother's," Mom responded. "Do you know where the homeschoolers are meeting?"

"Aha, a new victim!" the mom said. "Our ragtag band is over by the play structures."

The woman's name, she said, was Karma, and she seemed to talk as big as she was, with wide gestures and big smiles. As they walked toward the play area, she told them about her friend Rachel, who had a daughter Molly who was about Hanna's age.

Karma had a nine-year-old boy named Carlton. She pointed at him when they got to the benches. He was hanging upside-down and howling and beating his chest.

"He does that a lot lately," Karma said. "But he's really not scary, Hanna. Do you want to go play with him?"

Hanna didn't want to answer. She snuggled into her mom's side as her mom sat to nurse David.

Hanna listened to her mom's voice purring out

of her body. They talked about homeschooling. Hanna's mom talked about moving in with Gram. Karma talked about moving here with her husband because he got a job here.

"I'm an exotic tropical fish stuck in a goldfish pond," Karma said, and Hanna's mom laughed.

Hanna peered out at Karma's tropical colors. She was more colorful than anyone else Hanna had seen.

Mom put David down in the sand with a shovel, so Hanna sat next to him and dug with her hands. The sand felt good, gritty and loose. Hanna squeezed her hands then released them, letting the sand pour out. Her hands had a sand pattern imprinted in them.

A child came and stood over Hanna. He had short blond hair that looked like he'd cut it himself and he was wearing a shield made of aluminum foil and a sword made of spray-painted cardboard.

"Hark, yonder lady!" the child called out. "What is your appellation?"

Hanna peered up at the boy.

"Allow me to introduce myself," the child said. "I am Sir Lydia of Harkenfell. I am a valiant knight of the Kingdom of Win."

Hanna peered at the child again and figured that she must be a girl, even though she was dressed as a boy.

"Hi," she said.

"Come ye to our castle for fine vittles," Sir Lydia demanded.

Hanna cast a look to her mom. Sir Lydia spoke very strangely, but Mom smiled and nodded. Hanna stood up and followed Lydia to a space under the play structure where a few children sat. They were all talking in this funny way and each had a title: Sir Shawn, Princess Thea, and Sir Budgie.

"Who are you going to be?" Sir Lydia asked.

Hanna thought for a moment.

"I'll be King Hanna!" she said.

The other kids looked at each other doubtfully.

"I'll be a nice king," Hanna offered. "I'll be a king who bakes cookies."

"Hark!" Sir Lydia cried out. "King Hanna!"

Hanna felt a shadow fall on her and she looked up to see Karma's son, Carlton. He had his arms crossed and he didn't look too friendly.

"She can't be a king," Carlton said. "She's not big and brave."

Sir Lydia rolled her eyes. "Carlton thinks he can

decide everything for everyone," she said.

David fell asleep as soon as their car pulled away from the park.

"Oh, thank goodness," Hanna's mom said.

Hanna was quiet. She was thinking about all the things she would have to do as king. And she thought Carlton was kind of scary, though she didn't want to tell her mom.

"Did you like those kids?" Hanna's mom asked after they drove down Estates Blvd. and onto the freeway.

"Yes," Hanna said. "They have their own kingdom. They talk sort of funny."

"Ah, Karma told me about that," her mom replied. "They have a history class at Karma's house where they are learning about knights. Would you like to go?"

"What's a history class?" Hanna asked.

"They learn about things that happened in the past and make things. Karma says last week they made those cardboard swords."

Hanna thought it sounded like fun, though she wasn't sure about Carlton.

"Would I still have to be king?" she asked.

"You're the king?"

"I sort of said I would be," Hanna admitted. "I promised to give them cookies every time I see them."

Hanna's mom laughed. "That could get expensive. Perhaps you could just be king once a month."

Hanna said she thought that was a good idea.

When they got home, it was already after school, and Kira and Cassie's cars were in their driveways.

"Let's get the clay out," Hanna's mom suggested as she let David out of his carseat.

Hanna cast another look across the street. "OK," she said.

While Hanna's mom made dinner, Hanna made a clay castle while David banged on his lump of clay with a plastic hammer. Hanna's castle had a flag, a short-legged horse, and three windows. One of the windows was the king's bedroom, which had a four-poster bed and a quilt made by Gram, Hanna decided.

When it was time to set the table, Hanna rolled the whole castle up into a ball and watched the colors streak together as she twisted and pulled.

Chapter 4

Dad didn't have school on Fridays, so he usually spent a couple of hours with David and Hanna while Mom and Gram went to the store to do the week's shopping. On this Friday morning, Dad had a headache from being up so late and David was grumpy, too.

Hanna asked if she could go to the store with Mom and Gram.

"Only if you don't get the BMGM's!" Mom said with a grin.

BMGM meant "buy me, get me," which is what Mom said Hanna couldn't stop saying when they were in a store. Hanna didn't think she did it so much, but Mom made her promise not to do BMGM's even if they were just going in to get some milk.

"No BMGM's, I promise," Hanna said.

"No candy?" Mom said.

"No candy!" Hanna promised.

"No goldfish crackers?"

"Nope!"

"No magazines?"

Hanna had to think about this one. The grocery store stocked Ranger Rick, which Hanna really liked. It reminded her of living in the mountains.

"Well…"

"When we visit Carole in the winter she promised she'd give us all of Henry's," Mom reminded Hanna.

The winter seemed so far away, especially in a place where every single day was the same.

"Oh… OK," Hanna said. "No BMGM's at all. Please?"

Hanna was always amazed at the supermarket near Gram's. It seemed to be big enough to fit a whole neighborhood into. Gram had a special tag so they got to park right out front, which was good. The parking lot was as big as a forest but much more confusing.

Mom asked Hanna to get a cart from the row of carts nestled together in front of the store. The cart was stuck and when Hanna pulled, all the other carts wanted to come with it. Hanna stopped to look at it, puzzling it out.

"Let me help," Gram said from behind Hanna. Hanna saw that she got one cart to come out by jerking very hard so that the other carts let go. Hanna had been pulling strong and steady, which wasn't working.

Hanna saw Gram give Mom a look. Sometimes they sent these looks to each other that Hanna was sure were actually little arguments, but she couldn't prove it. Mom just answered with a smile that didn't show in her eyes.

Inside the store, Gram unfolded the list that she and Mom had put together and put it onto the seat where Hanna sometimes got to ride before she was too big to lift. Mom picked up the list and consulted it.

"Hanna, will you please go get one gallon of the milk we like?"

Hanna was about to say yes—this had been her favorite game in the little grocery store in the mountains. But Gram interrupted her.

"Jennifer," Gram said in a stern voice. "Do you think that is wise?"

Mom looked at Hanna and raised one eyebrow in a look Hanna thought was very funny. "What do you think, Hanna?"

Hanna was about to answer that she was very good and wise when it came to finding milk in a grocery store, but Gram interrupted her.

"I didn't ask your daughter," Gram said to Mom.

Mom sighed.

"Mom, Hanna is seven. And you know what I think about giving children meaningful jobs—"

"In this store full of strangers?" Gram asked.

Just then, two women waved at Gram, and a young man bagging groceries said, "Good to see you this week, Mrs. Cagan."

Mom said a loud "hmph!" and turned to Hanna.

"Hanna," she said. "Gram and I are going to that aisle on the left of the store and we'll work our way to the other side of the store. Please go find the milk we like and bring it to us, OK?"

Hanna nodded, trying to look serious and important as she figured Gram wanted her to look. She knew what this argument was about. Gram wanted to treat Hanna like a baby who couldn't do anything for herself. She didn't like Mom asking

Hanna to load the dishwasher because Hanna didn't do it exactly right. And she didn't want Mom to send Hanna on errands because she thought Hanna wouldn't get the right things.

But that was a silly thing to think. Hanna found their milk with no problem and carried it sloshing in her arms back to Mom and Gram, who were in the cheese aisle discussing something with their heads together.

"Thank you, Hanna," Mom said as she took the milk.

Hanna looked to Gram. "Is there anything else on the list I can get, Gram?" she asked.

Gram raised her eyebrows, sighed, tossed a look to Mom, and pointed. "Cream cheese?" she said.

That was so easy. It was just down the aisle. Hanna got the size they always bought and brought it back. All Gram said when Hanna put it in the cart was, "Thank you, dear."

Hanna wondered how big she would have to be before Gram would think she was big enough to do things herself. It seemed like Gram didn't think that Mom was big enough yet, even though Mom was bigger than Gram.

It was a puzzle, Hanna thought. Mom seemed

like a grown-up, till they moved in with Gram. And now Gram seemed to think Mom was her child again.

That afternoon Mom and Hanna made the challah, the traditional braided bread that Gram liked. They made it almost every Friday, now that they lived with Gram. They also lit candles every Friday at sundown and Gram said prayers in Hebrew.

Hanna had written out the recipe on a big sheet that Mom put in the cookbook holder. She thought it was funny that "challah" had a silent "c." It should be spelled HAH-LAH, Hanna thought.

Mom asked Hanna to give her the measuring cups she needed for two and three-quarters cups of flour, and asked her how she could make three-quarters with a different cup.

Hanna liked this game. She could make three-quarters of a cup with three scoops from a quarter cup measure, or a half plus a quarter. She could make a one cup from two half cup measures, three third cup measures, or a half and two quarters. Every week she got to choose how to do it.

Then she got to choose whether the two

teaspoons of yeast would be measured with two
scoops of a teaspoon or four scoops from a half
teaspoon. There wasn't, she pointed out to her
mom, a one-third teaspoon measure in their set.
How big would a one-third teaspoon be?

"That's a good question," Mom replied. "Let's
figure it out when we're done with the bread."

After the bread was in to rise, Mom let Hanna
measure a teaspoon of flour onto a cutting board
and split it into three equal piles as best she could.
Then they carefully pushed the one-third teaspoon
of flour back into the one-half teaspoon measure,
and Hanna saw that it was almost full.

"Almost, but not quite," Mom explained. "You
have to add one sixth to a third to get one half."

"One sixth is small!" Hanna said.

"Well," Mom pointed out, "It's small if it's one-
sixth of a teaspoon. Not so small if it's one-sixth of

an elephant."

"Or one-sixth of a garbage truck!" Hanna added.

"Or one-sixth of the planet Mars," Mom said.

"Or one-sixth of our solar system!"

Hanna had made the solar system out of paper disks stuffed with napkins. She made a big, yellow sun that felt hot to look at, and each planet with its color and size. They were planning to string it all together as a mobile and hang it over the dining room table from the chandelier. Hanna wondered whether Gram would like that addition to her *tschatschkes*.

Hanna heard David giggling from the living room. Dad had taken a nap and got over his headache. Gram was doing the crossword puzzle. Mom had a streak of flour on her cheek.

"I like Fridays," Hanna said.

"So do I," said Mom.

Hanna looked out the window across to Kira and Cassie's houses. But she didn't care at all that there wasn't time to go over and play.

Chapter 5

After a few times playing in the park with the other homeschoolers, Mom and Hanna decided to try out Karma's history club.

"Do I have to be king?" Hanna asked, thinking about all the cookies she'd have to bake.

"Definitely not," Mom said. "Karma says at their house, the dog is king."

The dog turned out to be an enormous black and white shaggy beast named King. Karma said she didn't bring him to the park because he got jealous that he wasn't allowed to dig in the sand.

When Hanna put out her hand for King to sniff, he schlurped her with such a kiss she had to wipe her hand on her dress.

All the kids from the park were there. Mom apologized for being late. "Ever since I had the second baby, I've never been on time," she said.

"The only reason I am on time is it's at my house!" Karma said with a laugh. "Come in!"

Karma's house looked like all the houses on her street, which were grey, light brown, or light blue with little porches and one scraggly tree on a small piece of lawn. But inside it was all just like Karma.

There was no adult-size furniture. People were supposed to sit on big pillows or the bright rugs that were thrown everywhere over the wall-to-wall, baby blue carpet. In the back yard there was a trampoline, which all the kids ran to right away.

Today Molly, the girl Karma had mistaken Hanna for, came too. Molly did look like Hanna, so much that their moms laughed. They both had straight brown hair bobbed short just under their ears so they wouldn't have to brush it. The difference was that Molly had her mom's brown eyes, and Hanna had her dad's blue eyes.

"Molly looks like she should be my daughter!" Mom joked to Molly's mom Rachel. Hanna liked how Molly and her mom's brown eyes looked warm and friendly.

Molly asked Hanna, "Do you like Pony Friends?"

"I don't know," said Hanna.

"Poor Hanna," Mom said. "We've never had a TV."

Hanna thought Mom was probably joking, because she knew Mom didn't like TV.

Molly's mom Rachel shook her head. "I try, but when I'm at work the sitter lets her watch all sorts of junk."

"I like Pony Friends because I can brush their tails," Molly said. "Do you want to jump on the trampoline?"

Molly showed Hanna how to jump holding hands, calling out moves so they'd do the same things each time. "Knees!" Molly would call out, and they'd bounce on their knees.

"Scissors!" Hanna called out and they scissored their legs as they jumped.

Soon Karma called them to some blankets she'd spread out under the tree and they sat in a circle. The moms sat on the patio and knitted and chatted, and there were tubs of soapy water and sand for the little children to play with.

Karma first read a story about a king named Arthur. He had a round table where he ate with all his knights, and they went out and had adventures. It seemed like the kids had all heard about him before, because they knew all the knights' names and they asked questions and answered each other's questions.

Every time Karma read the name Lancelot in the story, Carlton got up and ran around the circle, waving his homemade sword. Everyone laughed, but Hanna was afraid he was going to hit her with his sword.

Karma had to keep asking Carlton to sit down, and finally she took his sword from him. Then Carlton climbed up in the tree, which worked out better because Karma could finish the story.

After the story, the kids went into the kitchen to work on their castles. Hanna got a box that Karma had saved for her, and Karma showed her how to cut a drawbridge and attach strings, and how to make parapets out of construction paper. She gave Hanna a can to glue on as a tower.

The other kids had built their castles the last time they met, so they were painting theirs. Hanna liked how Molly was doing hers with small, careful strokes. Molly had even drawn bricks on the walls and made a window.

Hanna thought she'd like to make hers just like Molly's.

Then before she knew it, she was alone on the floor and the other kids were running around outside. Hanna's castle was ready to paint, but Mom said they were out of time.

"David's getting fussy, love," Mom said. "Let's get in the car and he can sleep."

Hanna felt an ugly lump of anger in her belly. Why did they always have to do what David needed to do?

"No!" Hanna said. "I won't! I want to paint like everyone else did."

Karma was busy cleaning up the paints. She put them in a box and sat down next to Hanna.

"You know you can paint next week," she said to Hanna.

But Hanna knew that they were planning to make people for their castles next time, and if she didn't finish now, she'd always be behind.

"No," she said. "I want to paint now."

Why didn't grown-ups see when things were important? Hanna felt hot and mad inside.

David was fussing and struggling in her mom's arms.

"Go on out, JJ," Karma said to Hanna's mom.

Hanna could feel tears in her eyes and she

didn't want to cry. Sometimes getting really, really mad could keep the tears from coming.

"No!" she shrieked as Mom carried David out.

But the tears came anyway, and she felt Karma's arm go around her and hug her.

"I know exactly how you feel," Karma said. "I never want to stop when I'm enjoying something. Sometimes little brothers need your mom's attention, though."

"I hate him!" Hanna said. "He always gets her attention!"

It felt really good to say that, but she could feel the tears melting her anger away.

"You can take your castle home and paint it," Karma suggested. "And when you come back you'll be all caught up."

"I want to paint it just like Molly's," Hanna said.

"Hers is beautiful," Karma agreed. "And yours will be, too. Do you want to bring some paints home or use your own?"

Hanna remembered that they had a new box of paints that Gram had bought, which Hanna was saving for a special project. She wiped the hem of her dress across her face.

"I have new paints," she told Karma. "When I get home, I'll open them up."

Hanna felt that hot ball of anger spread out and fizzle through her fingers. She felt very, very tired.

A few days later, Hanna stood looking at her castle on the sideboard. She opened the drawbridge and peered in. The castle was still unpainted. On the side, it said Fresh Kiwi Fruit. The can that was the tower had been a hot chocolate container.

David had been up half the night last night so Mom was tired. She asked Hanna to play quietly while she and David napped. Gram was out at her friend's house for tea and dominoes. Dad was at a class, as usual.

Hanna went to the recycling bin and found some newspaper. She knew that her mom was always pleased when she followed the rules and was responsible. She spread out the paper on the kitchen floor, found the new paints in their colorful box, and got some paintbrushes.

Her castle was not going to be like Molly's. It was going to be every color of paint. It wasn't going to be King Arthur's castle. It was going to be a rainbow fairy's castle. It had pink swirls of smoke up the sides of the walls. It had sequins that Hanna found in the art supplies drawer in Gram's sideboard.

As soon as she heard the sound, the first thing Hanna thought of was her empty stomach. It was growling empty. It was the emptiness that made her head feel crazy and light.

She sat back to look at her work. It was definitely the right castle for a rainbow fairy.

She heard the sound again.

"How did this happen?"

It was Gram, and she was not happy.

Hanna came out of the kitchen as Mom wandered in carrying David. Gram was standing in the dining room with her hands on her hips. Hanna followed Gram's eyes, and saw drips of paint on the floor and carpet, and handprints of pink, blue, green, and yellow on the sideboard.

How did that happen?

"How did this happen, Hanna?" Gram demanded.

Mom put David down and followed the trail of paint drips back into the kitchen. Hanna just sat and stared at the paint mess while Gram followed

Mom into the kitchen.

"What a beautiful castle!" Hanna heard Mom exclaim. "Did you paint this castle all by yourself, Hanna?"

Hanna knew that Mom liked her to be independent, but she also knew that Gram was very angry.

"It's a rainbow fairy castle," Hanna explained in a small voice.

Gram's face was drawn up tight.

Mom sighed and put her arm around Gram.

"I think maybe you have something to say to Gram," Mom said.

Hanna glanced back at the drips of paint that showed her path through the house.

"I'm sorry," she said.

Gram sighed again.

"I think Hanna will be very happy to help clean up," Mom said.

"Yes, I'll help!"

Gram just said "help" in a very grim way.

Mom said, "Hanna is such a great helper."

After dinner, Dad went with Hanna to run her bath and hear about her day. She told Dad about

Carlton and how he could never sit down.

"Some kids are like that," Dad said.

"He's a little scary," Hanna admitted.

"Well, you know your mom and Carlton's mom are there to help if you are worried about anything," Dad said.

"Karma says Carlton is a monkey in boy's clothing," Hanna said with a giggle.

After her bath, Hanna went to the top of the stairs in her pajamas. She could hear Gram and Mom talking.

"I hope you know what you're doing," Hanna heard Gram say.

Hanna thought that was a strange thing to say. Gram was talking to Mom the same way she talked to Hanna, like Mom wasn't a grown-up. But Hanna didn't think you could have children and not be a grown-up, so Gram must be confused.

When I'm a grown-up, Hanna thought, I'm definitely not going to live with Gram.

Chapter 6

When Kira brought over the invitation to her birthday party, Hanna thought it must have been a long time since she'd seen Kira and Cassie.

Things had gotten so busy. They had history class at Karma's house and art group at the community center and Gram had bought Hanna swim lessons, and many days Hanna and her mom went for a long walk, drew pictures, and talked about things.

By the time Kira and Cassie got back from school, Hanna was "all played out" and just wanted to read or listen to books on tape.

The invitation said "You're invited!" on the front and had a cartoon character Hanna had seen in the grocery store.

"I'm going to have a bounce house!" Kira said. "And chocolate cake!"

Hanna thought back to her own seventh birthday, which happened right after they moved into Gram's house and didn't know anyone. She had a cake and a few presents and Henry had sent her a homemade card in the real mail. The envelope was big and lumpy because he had glued acorns to the card.

But she hadn't even thought to ask for a bounce house. She never knew anyone who'd gotten one for her own party before.

"Can you come?" Kira asked excitedly.

"Yes," Hanna said. "I have to ask my mom."

Kira was bouncing with excitement. "It's going to be so much fun!"

Kira's party was on Saturday. Dad was home and said he'd play with David so that Mom could spend some time getting to know the other moms in the neighborhood.

"It's funny that we're homeschooling and we don't know anyone near home," Mom said to Dad.

Hanna had spent all morning making a pretty card for Kira. She knew Kira liked princesses, so she made the most beautiful princess, with glitter in her hair, standing by a big castle.

An enormous, loud bounce house was raised in Kira's back yard. It was a puffy castle. Kira was inside bouncing with Cassie and another girl Hanna didn't know. Kira was wearing a complete princess outfit including a crown.

Hanna joined in bouncing, and soon lots of other kids appeared one by one in the doorway to the bounce house.

After a while it got too crowded and Hanna went to find Mom.

The yard was filled with parents standing or sitting on plastic chairs, holding drinks and talking to each other. Hanna saw that Mom's back was to her. She was talking with three other moms.

Hanna crawled under the table that was behind the moms. It had drinks on it and a big white tablecloth. Inside, it felt very cool and large, not stinky and crowded like the bounce house.

"Oh, we spend so much time with other children of all ages," Hanna heard Mom say. "She has classes and play groups. We probably spend too much time socializing."

Hanna could hear the look on Mom's face. It was the same look she got when Gram said something critical. It was this patient, annoyed smile

that Mom got. She never did that smile to Hanna, though sometimes she did it to Dad when he said something she didn't like.

"But how can she learn to be independent?" the woman asked. "I think my kids need time away from me."

"And I need time away from them," another voice said.

A few voices laughed, but Hanna didn't hear Mom's laugh.

Just her patient voice, saying, "I think you'd be surprised. Hanna is probably more independent than most kids because she spends very little time in a group following directions. She has to make decisions for herself."

That's right, thought Hanna. I can make decisions for myself.

The decision she made just then was that listening to Mom's conversation was even worse than the bounce house full of kids.

She crawled out from under the tablecloth and saw that Cassie was doing the monkey bars. As she ran over, Cassie reached the last rung.

"Wow," Hanna said. "You can do the monkey bars all the way across."

"Of course I can," Cassie said, as if she didn't remember that she could only do three the last time they had counted together. "Can't you?"

"I haven't really tried," Hanna admitted.

"All the girls in my class can do it except Jessie. She's retarded," Cassie said.

"Oh," Hanna said. She didn't know what retarded meant, but it sounded bad. "Can you show me how you get across?"

Hanna thought Cassie was going to say something mean. She looked at Hanna like she thought Hanna was retarded, whatever that was. But then she shrugged and smiled.

"You have to throw your whole body," Cassie said. "Like this."

Just as Cassie was climbing up to show Hanna how to do it, Kira's mom banged on a big bell and yelled, "Cake time!"

That was all it took to empty out the bounce house.

The cake was a castle, too, and it tasted funny. Hanna took a bite and then didn't know what to do with the rest.

"Are you tired, Hanna?" Mom said, coming up and tugging on the back of Hanna's hair like she always did. "Ready to go?"

Hanna suddenly felt very heavy and very ready to go.

"Say thank you to Kira and her mom," Hanna's mom instructed.

Hanna did say thank you to Kira, though she didn't think Kira heard her. She was in the midst of tearing open a pile of gifts all wrapped in fancy paper with bows.

Hanna's mom was talking to Kira's mom. "Parties are so tiring!" she said. Hanna and her mom said goodbye, then walked out the open gate toward their house.

"Mom, what is retarded?" Hanna asked as soon as they'd cross the road to Gram's nice lawn.

Mom said, "Where did you hear that?" in a way that made Hanna think perhaps it wasn't something she was supposed to say.

"Cassie said a girl in her class is retarded," Hanna explained.

"Oh, Hanna," Mom sighed. They stopped in front of the house. "Some people are born with brains that have trouble working, just like some people are born with legs or eyes that have trouble working. But you know that doesn't make them less important as people."

Hanna hadn't thought that. She just wondered what it was.

"I know you know that," Mom said. "Anyway, some people use mean words for people who are different than they are. 'Retarded' is a not nice way of saying that someone's brain has trouble learning in the same way as other people's brains."

Hanna thought about that. She wondered what that had to do with doing monkey bars all the way across. She thought maybe that the girl just hadn't had time to learn. Hanna hadn't had time to learn, either.

"OK," she said to her mom.

Tuesdays were the only day that Cassie and Kira didn't have any after school activities. That Tuesday, Hanna watched at the window till Cassie got home, then went over to her house to ask her for another lesson on the monkey bars.

Kira and Cassie were sitting on Cassie's swings when Cassie's mom pointed Hanna to the back yard.

"Hi," Hanna said.

"For my birthday," Kira said, "I got two Barbies, a gift certificate to the movies, and a mermaid art kit."

"And a nail salon kit," Cassie added.

Hanna remembered that big pile of presents.

Kira fixed Hanna with a mean look.

"All you gave me was a dumb homemade card," Kira said. "Retard card!"

Kira and Cassie giggled.

But it had a princess on it, Hanna wanted to say. And a big rainbow castle. And I worked on it for a long time.

But she didn't know what she should say, so she

said nothing at all. She knew that all the other kids had brought big, fancy presents, and she had not.

Hanna stood there, because there were only two swings and she was the odd one out.

That evening, Dad was home before bedtime, and that meant he got to be the one to tuck Hanna in and sing her a song. He sang her "Be My Friend," a song they liked to sing up in the mountains. Dad was wearing his blue scrubs from the hospital, and his blue eyes looked tired.

"Why are some kids mean, Daddy?" Hanna asked.

Dad was sitting on the edge of the four-poster bed, holding Hanna's hand.

"Well, in my experience, kids are usually mean when they feel bad about themselves."

"What do you mean?" Hanna asked.

"Well, imagine you are is afraid that kids won't like you. So you think that if you do something mean to another kid, then that shows other kids that you are strong. But it really just shows them that you're afraid."

"That's a little weird," Hanna said.

"It is," Dad agreed. "But it seems to happen a

lot. Is someone mean to you?"

Hanna wondered if it was tattling to say anything, but she thought it would be OK.

"Sometimes Kira and Cassie aren't so nice," she admitted.

"Then why do you play with them?" Dad asked.

That was the sort of question Dad asked. His questions had an obvious answer, even when it seemed like there was no answer at all.

"I don't know," Hanna said. "They're interesting."

"Hm, what's interesting about them?" Dad wondered.

"They go to school," Hanna said.

Dad laughed and pinched her cheek. "Most kids go to school, Hanna-bug," he said.

"I know," Hanna said. "But I like to find out what school's like."

"Do you want to go to school?" Dad asked.

"I don't think so," Hanna said. "I thought maybe I did but I think that the other kids would call me retarded if I couldn't do the monkey bars like them."

"Well, Hanna-bug," Dad said. "No matter where you go there are nice kids and mean kids, and a lot of the mean kids are just mean because they're afraid of being nice, you know? I bet some homeschoolers are mean sometimes, too. Like, you're not so comfortable with Carlton, right? There would probably be some of both at school."

"So why don't I go to school?" Hanna asked. It seemed to Hanna like everyone was always saying bad things about homeschooling, except for the people who did it.

Dad thought for a minute. He squeezed Hanna's hand.

"Mom and I want you to be happy," he said. "Are you happy?"

"Yes," Hanna said.

"Mom and I think that homeschooling is better for you right now. More fun. In school you'd have to do a lot of worksheets."

"I know," Hanna said. "Kira and Cassie have homework."

"Well, if you want homework, you can always ask your mom," Dad said. "Do you feel like you have friends?"

"Yes," Hanna said. "Everyone in the history club plays together. I think Molly might be my friend."

"Well, if you have friends and you are enjoying

learning, that sounds pretty OK to me."

"I don't know if Gram thinks it's right," Hanna said. "She's always asking Mom these questions."

Dad cleared his throat. "Your grandmother is a woman with her own opinions. Just like her daughter—your mom!"

Hanna giggled. "I know," she said. "Sometimes they argue."

"That's pretty normal," Dad said. "It doesn't upset you, does it?"

"Nope," Hanna said. "They always end up happy."

"Exactly," Dad said. "That's what matters. Are you ending up happy tonight?"

Hanna sat up and gave her father a big bear hug. "Yes!" she said into his shirt, which smelled of the hospital. "Happy as pie."

chapter 7

O ne day Dad was home from school, and he said since he'd just taken tests, he didn't have any studying to do.

"What would you like to do with me?" Dad asked Hanna.

So many things went through Hanna's mind, she couldn't choose one. When they were in the woods, they did a lot of carpentry. From when she was three, Dad let Hanna use a small hammer and a real drill—with help. But there was no scrap wood pile at Gram's house.

They also went on tromps through the woods. When there was deep snow, Dad would throw Hanna into drifts that would catch her like enormous, cold hands. But there was no snow at Gram's house.

In the mountains, Dad drove a furniture

delivery truck, and sometimes he could take Hanna along. As they drove he would tell her stories, and the people at the houses often gave her little gifts. Dad said that people were always happy to get their furniture and be entertained by Hanna as he worked.

But here Dad went away to the college and sat in classrooms. Hanna couldn't go because a lot of his classes were at night and they were very long. And when Dad was working, he was learning to be a nurse in the hospital, where he worked doing the little jobs that nurses didn't have to do, like changing sheets on beds.

"Can you show me the hospital where you work?" Hanna asked.

"Hm," Dad said, putting on his thinking face. "We can certainly go there, but, well, yes!"

Dad broke into a big grin that told Hanna he had an idea.

Dad rummaged in the front hall closet and pulled out his guitar case. Dad used to sing songs pretty much every evening until he started studying to be a nurse. The guitar looked like an old friend from the mountains.

"Hang on while I tune this," Dad said to

Hanna, "and then we'll go do some nursing for the soul."

Dad parked in an enormous parking lot. The hospital seemed to be blocks away, past row after row of cars.

"Are there lots of sick people, Daddy?" Hanna asked. She felt shy and nervous. She didn't know why Dad needed a guitar for nursing, but she knew that something interesting was going to happen.

"Yes, Hannie," Dad said. "There are always lots of people in the world who are sick, but luckily, we live in a time when they can get better."

Dad had told Hanna a lot about the old days, when people got diseases they don't get anymore. He was proud that he was going to be a nurse, learning science and helping people at the same time.

They went through an enormous revolving door in the front of the hospital. Dad said it was big enough for a wheelchair. In the lobby of the hospital, there was a desk manned by a nurse all in white. She had deep chestnut-colored skin and hair in braids, and she spoke with a beautiful, lilting accent and a wide smile.

"Hello, Robert, my favorite nurse!" she called out.

Dad introduced her as Françoise and told her that they were going to do some nursing for the soul after he showed Hanna some of the hospital.

"We can't go in the parts where there are really sick people," Dad said. "But you'll learn a lot just by sitting here for a while and watching."

The hospital seemed a lot calmer, sunnier, and more pleasant than Hanna had expected. Dad had told her about hectic evenings when it seemed like everyone had broken a leg or had a heart attack. But today people came in and checked in with Françoise, and people were wheeled in wheelchairs across the lobby.

Françoise gave Hanna a book made just for children who had to stay in the hospital, all about how a hospital works. It had photos of children with tubes in their noses and children getting casts.

After a while, Dad said it was time to do some nursing of the soul. They said goodbye to Françoise and went back out the huge, revolving door. They walked all the way around the hospital, through the big back parking lot, and up to a low building with a fountain in front of it.

A big sign at the front said "Del Ray Convalescent Home." Hanna read it slowly aloud and Dad told her that "convalescent" meant people who had been sick and needed to get better. It was also a place for old people who needed so much nursing they couldn't live at home anymore.

There was a receptionist here, too, but she didn't look so friendly. She had big piles of paper on her desk and a look on her face like Dad and Hanna were bothering her.

Dad explained that they were here to sing to the people who lived here. Would it be OK if they went into the community room and sang for a while? The woman started to say no, but just then another nurse came in and she recognized Dad.

It seemed like people really liked Dad wherever he went. Hanna thought maybe it was the twinkles in his blue eyes or the soft blond beard that made him look more like a mountain man than a nurse. Even dressed in his scrubs for work, he never looked so official as the annoyed woman behind the reception desk.

Dad and Hanna set up in a corner of a big room where a few people were at tables playing cards. There were other people in wheelchairs, some talking but most just sitting. Almost everyone was old but one young man, who was in a wheelchair that held up his head so that he looked uncomfortable. He watched Hanna and Dad with angry eyes.

Dad had his fakebook, which was a folder full of the songs he had been singing since before Hanna was born. Before he met Mom and had Hanna and David, Dad liked to travel around singing. He had a van that he and his friends traveled and slept in, playing music wherever they could.

But Dad and Hanna didn't really need the book. Hanna knew the words to many songs. And the ones she didn't know, she could clap her hands or just listen and repeat things that Dad sang with a nod to her.

They sang He's Got the Whole World in His Hands for a warm-up, then Greensleeves, Michael Finnegan, and Foggy Mountain Breakdown. They sang funny songs and sad songs and marching songs.

Mostly Hanna didn't look at the people because it made her feel shy, but after a while, she noticed that more people had walked or wheeled in, and that most of the people were listening and not talking anymore. Some of them were singing along.

Dad told the people that he was studying to be a nurse, and learning how to heal people's bodies. But he figured that just as important as healing bodies is healing injured souls.

"And that's where music comes in," he said. One of the women listening said, "Ay-men!" loudly and many in the audience laughed.

As they sang, Hanna cast a few shy looks at the young man in the uncomfortable looking wheelchair. A nurse had come in and turned him so he was looking at Hanna and Dad.

For their last song, they sang Shenandoah, which was Hanna and Dad's favorite song to sing together. Hanna knew all the verses, and some of the people did too, and they sang along.

When they were done and Dad was packing up his guitar, Hanna looked over at the young man in the wheelchair. There were tears rolling down his cheeks, and he had no way to hide them or wipe them off.

They walked across the enormous parking lot quietly. The day was coming to a hazy end.

"Daddy?" Hanna said. "We made that young man in the wheelchair cry."

Dad hugged Hanna close. "I know," he said.

"Did we make him sad?" Hanna asked.

Dad thought for a while. They reached their car and he set his guitar case down and sat on it. "I think we made him sad and happy at the same time," he said. "Do you understand that?"

Hanna nodded.

"It's sad that he is in a wheelchair and can't do the things he wants to do anymore," Dad said. "But he was happy to have music."

"Will he always be in that wheelchair?" Hanna asked. "He looked uncomfortable."

"Oh, Hannie," Dad said. "I don't think he was uncomfortable. People have an amazing way of dealing with whatever life gives them. I'm glad we could give him some music today."

"Can we go back sometime?" Hanna asked on the way home.

"Of course, Hanna," Dad said. He glanced to the backseat and smiled. "I miss having my little buddy next to me to help me do my job."

"But your new job is so much more important than delivering furniture," Hanna said, echoing something Mom had said to her.

"I think so, my friend," Dad said. "And you know how important that is to me."

*

When they got home, Hanna got out her art supplies and drew lots of pictures of guitars, singing, and the man in the wheelchair. Mom was making dinner, and Dad and Gram played in the living room with David.

Hanna asked Mom how to spell all the words just right, and across the top of one of her pictures she wrote, "Music, happy and sad."

chapter 8

December was so full it was blurry like a snow globe when you shake up all the snow. First came Chanukah, which had a silent C just like challah. Hanna invited the whole history class to her house for donuts and songs and making menorahs out of clay. Menorahs are special candle holders for nine candles.

Gram read a Chanukah story from a book she got when she was a little girl.

Molly and Rachel stayed for dinner because Molly's dad was working nights. Gram reminded Mom how to make potato pancakes and brisket, and said things like, "I'm not criticizing, but—"

And Hanna's mom laughed a lot. Molly's mom said now she'd never get the dreidel song out of her head.

"Dreidel, dreidel, dreidel, I made it out of clay!"

they all sang.

Kira and Cassie's dads decorated their houses with lights so bright Gram's living room glowed. Gram and Mom and Dad called "Happy holidays" out to their neighbors when they passed even though they didn't have a Christmas tree in their window.

"This is a time of year when everyone celebrates light and love no matter what sort of church they go to," Gram said.

Hanna and Mom were very cheerful because they were going back to visit the mountains as soon as Dad's exams were over. Dad was tired, but he was looking forward to it as well. He took time to change the oil in the car and say he wished they had enough money to buy better tires.

Then before they knew it, they were backing out of Gram's driveway, Gram waving goodbye and promising that her friends Mira and Joyleen would be checking on her every day.

As they drove away, Mom asked Dad if he thought Gram would be OK.

Hanna wondered if good things always came with worries, the way they seemed to lately.

As they started "up the hill," as Dad called it,

the sky darkened and a few flakes fell.

"I thought we'd beat the snow," Dad said to Mom. The flakes came down silently on the car and Hanna watched in amazement as if she'd never seen it.

"Look, David," she said. "Snow!"

"No!" David said.

Hanna giggled. "No," she said. "Ssssssnow!"

"K-no!" David repeated, trying to catch the flakes that fell on the window.

Pretty soon there were flashing lights ahead and Dad said, "Time for chains."

Dad pulled over on the wide area made for cars to stop for putting on chains. Hanna had helped him with the chains at their cabin in previous years, but Dad said it was too cold and too dangerous out there on the highway, so Hanna stayed snuggled up in a blanket. David had fallen asleep in his carseat with his head to one side, drooling.

Mom got into the driver's seat with the window open, letting cold and snow in as she and Dad got the chains on.

After a while they got going again, but the traffic didn't. Dad had the radio on, and he said they were stopping traffic because the storm had come on bigger than expected. The cars crawled along and then stopped. Dad turned off the engine and every once in a while ran the windshield wipers so they could see.

David woke and fussed, so Mom climbed in the back seat and nursed him. She gave Hanna the snack bag and Hanna and Dad traded ideas about what flavor each corn chip was.

"This one is strawberry—yum!" Dad said.

"This one is fireberry," Hanna answered, popping one in her mouth.

"This one is a fire engine!" Dad exclaimed as he crunched down hard and started jumping in his seat.

David looked up and stared at Dad in amazement. David's favorite thing, since he had seen a fire engine blazing past the park a few weeks before, was to point out fire engines, or any large red vehicle.

"Endin!" David said.

When the car crunched into Carole and Don's neighbor's driveway, Hanna was fast asleep. She thought, in her dreams, that she felt the car moving again. She remembered Mom climbing over her and back into the front seat.

The lights were on and Don was stomping over the yard from his house to let them in.

"We've got it all ready for you," Hanna heard Don say. Hanna remembered that they were staying at the neighbor's house—"housesitting," Mom called it.

Mom picked up David out of his seat, and Dad lifted Hanna out of hers like she was a big baby. She knew she could have walked, but she liked the feeling of being a little one in Daddy's arms again. She buried her face in Dad's jacket and breathed.

Hanna woke on a futon in an unfamiliar bedroom. There was a big bed next to her, and David was asleep in the middle of it. The bed was rumpled like Mom and Dad had slept on either side of him.

Hanna got up and noticed that she was still in her clothes, and they were light, flat-landers' clothes. She hadn't been able to bear putting on an itchy sweater when they left yesterday morning.

She wrapped herself in a blanket and wandered out of the room. This cabin was just like the one Henry lived in next door. The big room was warm and happy with a roaring fire in the woodstove. A big orange cat was curled up in front of the fire. Mom was cooking in the kitchen, which was at one end of the big room.

"There she is!" Mom said. "Good morning, sleepy."

She reached down and gave Hanna a big hug through her blanket.

"Are you ready for oatmeal?" she asked. "And hot chocolate?"

It felt just like a winter morning in their cabin, except that the house faced a big view of the valley, and the furniture was unfamiliar.

"It's just like our cabin, isn't it?" Mom said. "Except backwards. Dad said when he went to the bathroom he went out on the deck by mistake!"

"That would have been cold," Hanna said.

"It is cold, isn't it?" Mom said. "It's easy to forget, living down there in the flats."

Mom served Hanna some oatmeal, and Dad came in with snow all over his clothing. He'd been out snow-shoeing with Don.

"Henry's already up and ready for a snowball fight," Dad said to Hanna. "Are you ready?"

"Yes!" Hanna said, shoveling her way through the oatmeal.

The day was spent in the snow and then thawing out over at Carole and Don's house, which was like home away from home for Hanna. Carole and Mom were best friends, and Don and Dad liked to joke that Carole and Mom did everything together, right down to having babies three days apart.

So Henry had been Hanna's best friend from the first day that Mom brought baby Hanna over to meet newborn baby Henry. Until Hanna's family moved down to Gram's house, she had seen Henry almost every single day.

They spent the evening sitting on pillows in front of Henry's small Christmas tree, which was still alive and in a huge tub that they always used for the Christmas trees they dug from their yard. The tree was decorated with ornaments that Carole and Henry had made from natural things like pine cones and pressed flowers. Don was an expert whittler, when he wasn't busy being a carpenter, and he had whittled a nativity scene for the tree.

Mom told Carole all about Karma and the history club and how they were finally meeting some homeschoolers in Gram's town. Mom called Carole her homeschooling mentor, because it was Carole's idea that they should homeschool their kids. Mentor was a fancy word for teacher.

Carole poked fun at how Mom had been so scared of homeschooling at first. Mom's parents had sent her to a private school and then to a famous university.

Mom had told Carole, "We like school in our family!" but now she said that she loved homeschooling.

"I can't imagine sending my best girl off every day and not being part of her learning," Mom said.

"Do you like your new neighborhood?" Carole asked Hanna.

Hanna had to think about that. She liked some things. She liked being with Gram, who could be a little cranky but who knew so many things and talked so seriously with Hanna. She liked the walks they went on, and she liked Karma and most of the history club kids. She liked playing with Molly, though it wasn't as easy as playing with Henry, who seemed to know what she wanted even before she knew what she wanted.

Hanna knew that Carole wanted a real answer. Carole waited till people were ready to say what they had to say.

"I like living with Gram," Hanna said, and she noticed that Mom's eyebrows went up and Dad's eyes twinkled. "I miss Dad when he's away so much. I like history club. I like not being cold in winter but I miss the snow."

"Isn't that funny?" Carole mused. "Sometimes we get new things we like when we leave behind other things we like."

Hanna thought Carole knew a lot. Carole talked to Hanna like she knew a lot, too. Dad got his guitar out and they spent the evening singing Chanukah and Christmas songs. Hanna looked at the cloth-wrapped gifts by the tree and knew that one of them was for her. But even without gifts, it was as perfect an evening as she'd ever had.

chapter 9

One day in January Hanna asked a question, and the question turned into a fieldtrip.

Hanna had been thinking about all the farmland they'd driven through on their way back from the mountains. Up in the mountains nothing was growing—it was all under snow.

But down here in the valley, there were fields in every state of growth. The long rows of grapevines were now bare. When they were driving back, there were people in a field trimming long vines and throwing them in a truck.

Other fields were brown and empty. But some fields were green with winter rain and growing plants.

"What do they grow on those farms we saw?" Hanna asked.

As soon as Hanna asked her question, Mom

had the computer open and they looked up farms they could visit in the area. Then Mom e-mailed all their friends. Within a few days, Hanna was wearing rubber boots and standing in mud that sucked at her feet and was already all over David's hands.

"Welcome to Sally's Farm!" a woman said as she strode toward them. She wore high rubber boots, worn overalls, and had a little baby strapped to her back. The baby peered out at them with curious eyes. "I'm Sally and this is Marlow."

Almost the whole history class was there, including Molly, and a new family they'd met at the park had come along, too. They had two very big girls with long braids and shy smiles.

Molly grabbed Hanna's hand as they walked past the farmhouse, which had a friendly dog behind a gate, and down a path through the fields.

"Do you see all those huge fields of just one thing when you're driving on the highway?" Sally asked. "My farm is not that kind of farm. We grow food to sell directly to families. What do you think they'd do if one week all that was in their box was corn?"

"They'd grow ears in their stomach!" Carlton shouted out.

Sally nodded seriously, like Carlton hadn't made a joke.

"That's right," she said. "People can't live on just one thing. We grow all sorts of things, and each week our customers get a box full of vegetables and fruit for their whole week."

Sally led them into a small field bordered by a homemade fence. It had tumbling plants growing up rows of string stretched between stakes. At first Hanna and Molly didn't see anything, till Sally pointed out the many pea pods hanging from the plant.

Sally showed them how the plant would break if they grabbed and pulled. Each of them carefully plucked a pod from the plant and crunched on it. It was sweet and juicy. Even David chewed on one and didn't spit!

In another field, they saw big leaves and stubby places where the big leaves had been harvested. Sally called it "elephant kale" and that it was full of good vitamins.

In an orchard, they saw bare apple trees, lemon trees with fruit on them, and avocado trees with many heavy avocados. Sally picked an avocado for each of them and they were surprised at how hard and heavy it was!

"Soft avocados you buy in the store were picked a week before, at least," Sally explained. "They don't ripen on the tree."

Lemons, she showed them, started as little green buttons that came from sweet-smelling flowers, and they had to stay on the tree until they were completely ripe. Carlton grabbed at a tree branch and yelped! The trees hid curved, nasty-looking thorns.

Hanna could have told him that, because Gram had a lemon tree in her yard. It was no good for climbing, because of the thorns.

Sally showed them the compost pile, and explained that they put all the plant clippings there. They could see that there were lots of things on the pile on the left, like kale and weeds, and a whole bunch of bean plants that had to be pulled. But the next compost pile looked just like dirt.

Sally grabbed a big pitchfork and scooped a big hunk of the dirt onto the ground. She asked them to look closely at it.

Molly and Hanna pulled some of it apart with their hands and exposed a big, pink worm! Sir Budgie (wearing all his knight gear) found a roly-poly. Thea shrieked when she found what used to be a banana peel.

It wasn't dirt at all!

"What is it?" Sally asked.

"Worm poop!" Thea shrieked again.

"A house for beetles?" Carlton asked.

"Compost," said one of the shy, serious big girls.

"This," said Sally, "is the cycle of life."

In the car on the way back, Hanna thought about their fieldtrip. She didn't think it was anything like the fieldtrips that Kira and Cassie took with their school. Cassie had said she even got a worksheet for fieldtrips.

"Mom, why don't I get homework?" Hanna asked her mom as she watched David's head loll as he fell asleep.

"I guess everything we do is homework," Mom replied. "Except at history class."

"It's not the same," Hanna said. "Kira and Cassie get homework even when they go on fieldtrips. Like worksheets."

"Ah, worksheets," Mom said. "Well, I guess I could put something together. Would you like that?"

"Yes," Hanna answered.

When they got home, Mom went to nurse David for his nap. Hanna got out her drawing stuff and started a big picture on the long roll of paper. She started with a seed, and made a big arrow. Then she drew a little plant, and another big arrow. Next she drew a tree, and another arrow. Then a tree with lemons, and an arrow. Then a lemon.

"Gram?" Hanna called out to Gram, who was reading in her room. "What do you like to make with lemons?"

"When life gives me lemons," Gram called back with a smile in her voice, "I make lemonade!"

Hanna drew an arrow from the lemon to lemonade in the flower-painted ceramic pitcher Gram had. She sat back on her heels and thought for a minute. Then she drew another arrow from the lemon to a squished-up lemon. Then an arrow from the lemonade to a picture of Gram with a big smile on her face and a cup of lemonade. Then an arrow from the squished-up lemon to a compost pile with a big smiling worm in it.

Hanna sat back and felt like she was panting from running. This was very hard!

Then finally, she drew an arrow from the

compost pile to a pitchfork like Sally's full of dirt, then an arrow from the pitchfork to a new drawing of a lemon tree.

Mom came in then and told her how to write CYCLE, which she drew in big, careful letters. She knew how to spell OF and she thought she could get LIFE right because it had a sneaky silent E on the end.

Gram came out and she and Mom watched Hanna finish up her project.

"Wow," Mom said. "You worked so hard on that. How long is it?"

She winked at Gram.

Hanna ran to get the measuring tape from her sewing box.

The measuring tape stopped at 6 feet, and her drawing was still longer. Gram said, "You put your finger there on the end and then your mom can measure the rest. My bones are too old to get down on the floor!"

Hanna put her finger at the end of the measuring tape, and Mom brought the "0" end back over and started at Hanna's finger. She measured 9 inches more.

Hanna said, "So it was six feet long, and then

there were 9 inches more. What's that?"

Mom said, "Do you remember how many inches are in a foot?"

Hanna thought there were twelve and Mom said she was right. "So there isn't enough left to make another foot."

"Six feet, nine inches long!" Hanna said. "Can we hang it up?"

"Maybe we need to start learning metric," Mom said.

Then Mom went to get the tape and Hanna and Gram chose a spot on the long back sliding door. Mom started talking grownup talk to Gram.

"So you see, it starts with a question, then it becomes a fieldtrip, which creates an interest, which leads to a project, which depends on art, science, spelling, and math to be completed."

She taped the corners of the picture, and at the very end, Hanna wrote in her best numbers, 6 feet 9 inches, with Mom and Gram spelling feet and inches for her.

"That nine is backwards," Gram said.

Mom smiled. "It'll take care of itself in time, won't it Hanna-bug?"

Hanna was very pleased with her drawing. She

looked at her tree and added one more lemon. She counted nine lemons.

"Maybe you should give me nines homework," Hanna suggested, looking up at Mom.

"Well," Mom started like she was going to say no. "Why not?"

Mom made Hanna a worksheet on lined paper with neat, lightly drawn number nines at the beginning of each line. She handed Hanna the pencil and sat her at the kitchen table.

"Trace each nine, then write nines four more times on each line," Mom instructed.

Hanna looked at the sheet. She counted the nines Mom had made, then imagined five nines on each line. That was a lot of nines! But she was determined to do it. So while Mom made dinner, Hanna worked carefully, copying the nines onto her paper.

At the end, her hand hurt. And all she had was a page full of nines.

Hanna left the paper on the table and wandered out to look at her drawing, which was now glowing white against the dark outside. It was like a little bit of the fieldtrip brought home. She wandered back into the kitchen.

Mom was looking at the paper, David balanced on her hip.

"This is very good, Hanna. Did you enjoy doing it?"

"No," Hanna answered truthfully.

"Do you feel you learned anything?"

"Not really," Hanna said. "Well, maybe my nines will want to be right side around now."

"Would you like me to give you worksheets every night?"

Hanna looked at all the nines on the paper. "Twenty-five," she answered.

Mom's eyebrows made a question mark.

"Twenty-five nines," Hanna explained. "I don't think I need homework every day. I'd rather make up my own things."

"Well," Mom said with a smile, "you just let me know, OK?"

"OK," Hanna said. She took the sheet of paper and put it in the big folder Mom called her portfolio. The nines slipped in between two drawings and were swallowed up.

Chapter 10

Hanna particularly liked it when Gram's friends Mira and Joyleen came to visit.

They had a schedule: On Saturdays, Mira hosted mah-jongg at her house in the evening. Mah-jongg was a Chinese game they liked to play. Gram came home late, after Hanna was in bed. On Mondays, they all took a long, slow walk to the donut shop for what Dad called "bad coffee and good conversation." On Tuesdays and Thursdays they swam together at the heated pool where Hanna had her lessons. And on Wednesdays, they took turns hosting a get-together at each house.

Gram said she didn't know why Hanna liked hanging out with the grandmas, but Hanna loved to hear their conversation. Since her family had moved in with Gram, she and Mom always made cookies for Gram's teas, too. Gram liked that, because she had stopped doing much baking since her hands started to shake.

Mom usually took David out to the grocery store or the park when Gram's friends were home. Hanna would set up some work for herself on the dining room table so she could hear the women talk.

One rainy day they were in a particularly funny mood. Hanna thought that after knowing each other so long, they'd know everything about each other.

But today each one started telling funny stories about when they met their husbands. Hanna listened while she cut up a bunch of her old drawings to be confetti.

Joyleen was the only one whose husband was still alive. She called him "the Cranky Man" when she said anything about him to the others.

"You know," she said today. "He wasn't always the Cranky Man. When he was courting me Cranky Man wrote me limericks!"

Hanna knew that limericks were funny poems. Her dad had one that he'd turned into a song:

There was an Old Person whose habits,
Induced him to feed upon rabbits;

When he'd eaten eighteen,

He turned perfectly green,

Upon which he relinquished those habits.

Dad called that his "vegetarian song." Hanna couldn't imagine Cranky Man writing limericks that Joyleen would say out loud, but then Joyleen's voice spoke up strong and young, like she was eighteen again.

"There was a girl called Joyleen,

Whose hair smelled exceedingly clean;

She let Johnny kiss her,

And then he would miss her,

If he didn't marry Joyleen."

All the ladies laughed their merry laugh, which Hanna thought sounded like ringing bells. Gram's bell was deep and a bit hoarse. Joyleen's tinkled like a little bell on the doorway to a store. And Mira barked like one of those little dogs she had.

Mira said that she met her husband at a dance. It was for returning World War II soldiers and Mira said he looked so dignified in his uniform.

"If I'd known he was going to spend the next fifty years with his shirttails hanging out and a stain on his tie, I might have felt different that night!"

Again the women chimed their laughter.

"Your turn, Maggie."

Gram's voice was soft, and not as happy.

"Well, I grew up with Henry, you know. But after the war, we moved West and I didn't stay in touch."

She was speaking slowly and quietly. "I remember when Henry came back from the war. He'd been a prisoner of war."

Hanna knew some things about the war, but not much. She knew that a lot of people were killed and it was a very sad time for the country. She didn't know it was a sad time for her family. Grandpa Henry looked so calm and proud in the picture on Gram's dresser, wearing his uniform and looking so young.

"He could hardly talk. He was so thin. He said in the end they were digging for roots like pigs."

Hanna thought about what it felt like to dig in moist, cold soil. She imagined pulling up roots and tasting them. She thought they'd probably be bitter.

"Strangely," Gram's voice started up louder, "We didn't really have much feeling for each other. I was years younger, and our mothers were always arguing! My mother was thrilled that we were moving away from Brooklyn."

"We moved out West. My dad started his furniture store out here. He thought, all these young men coming back from the war, they'll want to get married and they'll need a bedroom set!"

The ladies tittered again.

"It was years—oh, my parents thought I was going to be an old maid!—years in which Henry went to college and applied for his job out here. No one in the old neighborhood sent news about him. Then one day, he came into the store. I hardly recognized that young man with his filled-out cheeks. Just like the war faded and our country moved into happier times, that was me and Henry."

All the ladies sighed and sipped their drinks.

"Happier times," Gram said again. "Of course, it took us many more years for our baby Jennifer to come into our lives. Mother said it was because I waited so long to get married."

"All's well that ends well," Mira said.

"Yes," Gram said, turning to smile at Hanna. "All's well."

Later, Hanna sat at the window seat and watched till Cassie's car pulled into the driveway.

She told Mom she was going out to play and ran across to Cassie's just as Cassie was coming out the back door with a muffin in her mouth. It was a sunny, mild day, the sort of day that said spring was coming.

Cassie's mom stepped out of the house behind her and waved to Hanna.

"Hello, Hanna! We haven't seen you in a while," she said. "How are you doing?"

"Fine," Hanna said. "Can Cassie play?"

"Sure, for a bit," Cassie's mom said. "She has homework."

Cassie made a face at Hanna. "Does your mom make you do homework?" she asked.

Hanna didn't really know how to answer that. She hadn't asked for homework since she did the nines, but she had put a lot more interesting things into her portfolio.

"I guess so," Hanna answered. "But I usually get to choose what it is."

"How interesting," Cassie's mom said. "Like what?"

Hanna considered today's learning. She wondered what her homework would be.

"Like today I wrote a limerick," she said.

"What's a limerick?" Cassie asked.

"Are you studying limericks?" Cassie's mom asked.

"Well…" Hanna said, not sure what she meant by 'studying.' "I guess I am. It's a poem. A funny poem. Like this."

She recited Dad's vegetarian song and Cassie's mom laughed. It made Hanna feel good that Cassie's mom got the joke. But Cassie seemed confused.

"Why is it called a limerick?" she asked.

"I don't know," Hanna said, looking to Cassie's mom.

Cassie's mom shrugged. "I guess you'll just have to ask your teacher," she said with a smile.

"Or you can look it up," Hanna suggested, just like Mom would.

That night, Hanna asked Dad and he started to tell her the story of limericks, complete with a funny Irish accent and all the silly limericks that he could still remember, in spite of stuffing his brain, as he said, with all that medical knowledge he was getting.

They got out Gram's big atlas and looked up Ireland and Gram said that once she and Grandpa had traveled there, and it was the greenest place you could ever imagine.

Then Dad danced a jig with David on his shoulders, bouncing and laughing. Hanna thought about asking Mom for limericks homework, but she decided to join the dance instead.

Chapter 11

Spring busted out of the plants so hard Hanna thought she should hear popping sounds. Gram had a big flowering crabapple in her front yard, which she called "the fanciest bride you'll ever see." Hanna could stand under the tree and hear the happy bees hum in the fluffy white flowers.

Molly missed her dad, too. He was working nights because his business had laid people off and he wanted to keep his job. Molly's mom had a job on Tuesday afternoons, so Molly stayed all afternoon and did projects with Hanna.

Molly really liked science, so Hanna's mom came up with all sorts of projects. They decided to call their Tuesday afternoons "Messy Camp." They made all sorts of mysterious goopy things, like ooblick that was soft and wet if you pressed on it slowly or really hard if you banged on it. They made a volcano out of papier mâché and the next week it exploded with baking soda and vinegar.

But the very best Messy Camp came to happen because David was being fussy and wouldn't go down for his nap.

Mom told Hanna and Molly that she was going to have to stay with David up in her room longer than usual to try to get him to nap. When David didn't get his nap, he was called Super Beast because he was so hard to deal with.

It was a warm, sunny afternoon, almost too hot but not quite. Gram was in her room with the window closed and the air conditioner on.

Hanna and Molly went out into the back yard and started making paint by grinding sidewalk chalk into containers. Molly got pink, orange, and yellow, and Hanna took green, blue, and purple. Grinding was hard work but satisfying as they watched the dusty piles of chalk accumulate in their containers.

Molly told Hanna about how she made paints with different plants, so they started picking leaves and rose petals from Gram's roses. They ran out of containers, so they dumped the chalk dust in piles on the patio, each color on a different square of

Gram's Spanish tile.

They put the rose petals in containers with a little water and ground the color out of the petals. Hanna remembered that one bush had just gotten little red berries, and they discovered that grinding those made a very satisfying deep purple color.

Then they started to paint. They painted the tiles. They painted the lawn furniture. They painted their feet, then their arms and legs, then each other's faces.

They made up crazy songs for what they were. Hanna was a deep sea monster and she roared and did a funny dance.

Molly was a giggling fairy who had a magic wand that brought plants to life.

It was a magical afternoon that stopped suddenly when Gram's voice said, "Oh, my goodness!"

Hanna and Molly looked to see Gram and Molly's mom Rachel standing at the sliding door, their eyes big.

Hanna looked around. Gram's orderly garden was changed. The Spanish tiles were painted different dusty chalk colors. Leaves and rose petals made a map of the dances that Hanna and Molly had done.

Hanna's hands were black with mud, turning grey as it dried.

Rachel started to laugh. Rachel had a full belly laugh that was contagious. When she laughed, everyone caught it.

But at first, Hanna and Molly were quiet, looking at Gram.

Then Gram started to laugh. She laughed till she coughed and then she laughed till she cried.

Hanna would have laughed, too, but she was a little scared that Gram would be mad at her.

Then Mom appeared behind Gram and Rachel with David on her hip. She looked confused.

"What's going on?" she asked. Her hair was mussed and she looked tired like it was the early morning.

"Your daughter," Gram managed to say before she broke into laughter again.

"What a mess!" Rachel managed to say, breathing hard before she was laughing again.

Finally everyone stopped laughing and Mom said, "I'm sorry, I must have fallen asleep with David." She turned to Gram. "And where were you?"

"There was a very interesting piece on the History Channel," Gram said, then she started to laugh again. "I had no idea."

Molly and Hanna both wondered if they'd done something wrong, but it didn't seem like it.

"Wow," Rachel said. "OK, you two maniacs, I'll get you cleaned up while Maggie and JJ figure out how we're going to feed ourselves."

Rachel started by getting out the hose and setting it on "shower." Molly and Hanna danced all the paint and dirt onto the patio. Their stamping bare feet made patterns on the tiles, as all the colors ran together as grey.

Then Rachel had them squeeze their clothes so they wouldn't drip as they went upstairs to the shower. Hanna had to lend dry clothing to Molly because hers were soggy and chalk-colored.

"I thought I knew crazy," Rachel said as she dried them off. "But I didn't know nothing till I saw you!"

Hanna caught Molly's eye and then it was their turn to laugh until they cried. Then Molly told Rachel all about which leaves and petals made good paint, and Hanna told Rachel about the deep sea monster and the giggling fairy.

It was one of Dad's late nights out, so Hanna, Molly, and Rachel came downstairs quietly to find

a table set by Gram for six. David was in his high chair, eating rice crackers. Gram said she was "sous chef" to Mom, helping her get dinner in half the normal amount of time.

Gram's shaky hands dropped a whole dish of olives, and she and Mom laughed and laughed as Mom found olives under all the counters and one in the bubbling pot of pasta.

Hanna thought this must have been the craziest day ever at Gram's house. Did Gram and Mom ever laugh so much when Mom was a little girl?

Hanna tried to imagine it, but Mom said that Gram had been pretty stern. That's the way parents thought they were supposed to be in those days.

After dinner Molly and Hanna cleared the table and even used the dustpan and brush to clean up under David's chair. Then they went outside into the cooling evening. The evidence of their dance was still everywhere on the patio, so Hanna got the push broom from the garden shed and she pushed while Molly sprayed. They got the whole patio clean and watered the plants at the same time.

"Do you have a best friend?" Hanna asked Molly.

Molly said, "I thought I did when I was in school last year, but after Mom took me out, my friend didn't call me anymore."

Hanna was surprised that Molly had gone to school.

"I had a best friend on the mountain," Hanna told Molly. "But I don't get to see him anymore. Now he's my longest friend instead of my best friend, because I knew him longer than anyone else."

"I guess I have a longest friend," Molly said. "My cousin Janna knew me since I was born, and she's my friend. But she lives in New Jersey, so we only see each other sometimes."

"Do you want to be best friends?" Hanna asked.

"Can we still be friends with all the other kids in the history club?" Molly asked. "When I had a best friend at school, she didn't want to play with anyone else."

"That sounds sort of mean," Hanna said.

"Yeah," said Molly. "I don't want to be mean."

"I think we can be friends with everyone. Even the ones we don't want to play with all the time."

"OK," Molly said.

"And we can still have our longest friends, too," Hanna said.

"We'll have them always," Molly said. "That's what Mom says is best about old friends."

The next day, Mom helped Hanna write a long letter to Henry. She told him about the fanciest bride tree, the chalk-painted dance, Gram's tea parties, and a song she and Dad had made up.

Mom did the writing because Hanna's ideas were coming out faster than her hands could work. David, who had learned how to walk, pulled on Mom's pants and said, "Nuss! Nuss!" which was what he said when he wanted to nurse, but Mom let Hanna finish the whole letter.

While Mom nursed David, Hanna drew pictures all over the letter and signed it in her best writing. At the bottom she wrote, "Molly is my frend. Henry is my frend."

Then she asked Mom how to spell "friend" and she was happy that the missing letter was a skinny one. She put in the i's and folded the letter carefully.

She imagined Henry sitting on his porch and the snow melting away. She remembered how there would be patches of it lasting well into the summer, and how the wildflowers would come up beside the snow like the mountain couldn't decide what season it was.

She remembered the smell of the little yellow flowers that came up all around their cabin. She went outside to smell Gram's roses, which were fancy, like the bride. But roses were no more beautiful than the little yellow flowers that nature made.

Chapter 12

One afternoon while Hanna and her mom were making muffins, David was taking his nap, and Gram was out with her friends, the phone rang.

Mom answered the phone and got a funny smile on her face.

"Of course," she said. "Here she is."

She held the phone out to Hanna.

"It's Cassie," Mom said. "For you."

Hanna thought it was very funny to receive a phone call this way. Though she sometimes dialed the phone for her mom, and often talked with someone who called, she had never even thought of asking to make a call. And Cassie was just across the street. She didn't even know Cassie's phone number, though she knew that Gram knew it because Gram kept the neighborhood phone list for emergencies.

"Hello?" Hanna said.

"Hi Hanna," Cassie said breathily, as if she had been running. "Can I come play at your house?"

This was more perplexing. One time when they had just moved in with Gram, Cassie and her mom came over and knocked on their door. And then there was the time that Kira brought the birthday invitation. But otherwise it was always Hanna who went over to their houses, and she hadn't done that in a long time.

Every time she thought of doing it, she thought of the yucky feeling she got when they were mean to her. Even when their moms were trying to be nice to her, they made her feel like she was so weird because she didn't go to school.

But Cassie had never been mean to Hanna when she was alone, just with Kira.

"Well, OK," Hanna said. "I have to ask my mom."

Hanna put the phone down on the counter. "Can Cassie come over?"

Mom's eyebrows went up like they did whenever she wanted Hanna to think about something she wasn't going to say.

"Do you want to play with her?" Mom asked.

Hanna nodded.

"Well, then, it's fine with me."

"OK," Hanna said into the phone. "You can come over."

She hung up the phone and saw her mom's eyebrows go up again.

"Oops," Hanna said. "Goodbye!" she said to the phone.

Mom laughed.

"OK, you're off duty once you've measured two and a half cups of flour."

Hanna watched out of the corner of her eye as she was measuring the first cup and saw Cassie and her Mom crossing the street.

"I'll let them in," Mom said.

Hanna listened hard to their voices through the wall as Mom let them in, but she couldn't understand the muffled words. Then they all came to the kitchen as Hanna was dumping the half cup of flour in.

"You let her measure?" Cassie's mom asked. "Does she know how to do it correctly?"

"Hanna's been helping me bake since she was big enough to hold a spoon," Mom said with a wink to Hanna.

"What are you making?" Cassie asked.

"Blueberry muffins," Hanna told her.

"Do you only make muffins in homeschool?" Cassie asked.

The grownups both laughed but Hanna could see that Cassie really meant it.

"Well," said Hanna. "Sometimes we make challah."

"And stew and pretzels and jam and soap and ooblick and wienerschnitzel, too!" Mom said.

"What's wienerschnitzel?" both girls asked at once, and the moms laughed again.

"Cassie is very excited," Cassie's mom said like it was a grand announcement. She put her hand on Cassie's head. "She graduated from kindergarten today!"

Hanna wondered what graduated meant. She knew that Mom said that they'd have a big celebration when Dad graduated from nursing school, but she didn't know what that would have to do with kindergarten.

"Kira got to go out to lunch with her grandparents," Cassie said. "They gave her lunch and her own ride-on Pony Friends electric car."

"Some people do make a pretty big deal out of

the last day of school," Cassie's mom said. "I'm just glad it's summer break."

That was another thing Hanna didn't know about.

"Cassie won't have to go to school for a couple of months," Hanna's mom said, as if she was reading Hanna's mind. "Are you going to camp, Cassie?"

"I don't know what I'd do with her if she weren't," Cassie's mom said.

"Swim camp, soccer camp, and art camp," Cassie counted off on three fingers.

"Sounds like you'll be very busy," Mom said with a kind smile.

"These days with all the cuts in the schools, I feel like we need to do a lot of enrichment," Cassie's mom said.

"School talk," Cassie said to Hanna, rolling her eyes. "Let's go."

Cassie and Hanna went out into the living room.

"Where's your room?" Cassie asked. "Where are your toys?"

Hanna thought about her room. It had books, and her stuffed animals, and it had the big puzzle that Don had cut with his jigsaw. It had all her collections from the mountains and the pressed flowers from Gram's yard. But she knew that Cassie was talking about bought toys, and she didn't have a lot of those.

"Do you want to do some coloring?" Hanna asked. "We have really big paper."

"OK," Cassie said with a shrug. "Do you have any coloring books?"

Hanna thought about that.

"I can make coloring books," she said.

"Oh, yeah, I do that sometimes," Cassie said.

She helped Hanna get out the big roll of paper and cut four big pieces. Then Cassie folded them together and Hanna got out Gram's big black stapler. She leaned down and stapled all along one side.

Hanna handed the book to Cassie, who giggled. "This is the biggest coloring book I ever saw!" she said.

"Let's make one for me, too," Hanna said. "What are you going to make a book about? I have been thinking about making a book about flowers."

"I think mine will be about princesses who are friends," Cassie said.

They worked together to make Hanna's book and then pulled out crayons, colored pencils, and markers.

Hanna drew an enormous rose on the front color and wrote R O S E below it. That was easy. Sneaky silent E.

"Mom?" she called out. "How do you spell flowers?"

Hanna's mom and Cassie's mom were still talking in the kitchen, but their voices stopped. They walked out into the dining room as Hanna's mom started to spell. "F L O W," she said, "E R."

Hanna wrote in big letters along the top, F L O W E R S.

"You forgot S," Cassie's mom said to Hanna's mom, and then she saw that Hanna had put the S on herself.

"I think Hanna's got plurals figured out," Hanna's mom said. "Except for those 'ES' ones."

The moms went out the sliding door. Cassie had started to work on her own book, drawing pictures of girl princesses holding hands.

"Kira isn't really friends with me anymore," Cassie said.

Hanna was surprised.

"She's friends with Charlene and Zoe," Cassie explained. "They're in first grade, too. They're mean."

Cassie drew a princess with long, yellow curls and a crown.

"I like your princess," Hanna said.

Hanna turned the page and folded it down over the staples. She knew what she wanted to do: She wanted to put all Gram's flowers into the book and give it to Gram as a gift.

She got a blue crayon and drew big blue swirls, then she put lots of green stalks beneath it.

Mom and Cassie's mom were talking on the patio. Cassie's mom was telling Hanna's mom how nice it was of a "big girl" like Hanna to play with Cassie.

Hanna looked at Cassie and she didn't seem so small.

"How do you spell hydrangea?" Hanna called out.

Both moms broke out in peals of laughter.

Later Hanna was eating another muffin at the table when she saw Kira's car pull in. Mom was feeding David a snack and trying to read Gram's

Good Housekeeping magazine, which she said was "insipid."

"What does 'graduate' mean, Mom?" Hanna asked.

Mom seemed to be interested in something in the magazine. It had pictures of a woman with long, blonde hair.

"Moving on," Mom said absentmindedly. "People graduate from college when they're done and they're getting their degree."

"Or kindergarten?" Hanna asked.

"Well," said Mom. "That's sort of a new thing." She smiled at Hanna. "Do you want to have a graduation?"

"From kindergarten?" Hanna asked. She actually didn't really know if she was in a grade. When people asked, Mom said that homeschooled kids didn't need grades.

"Hm," Mom said, putting on her thinking face. "I'd say you're more like first grade. And maybe like a baby because you're my baby!" she said in a funny voice.

Hanna groaned. "David's your baby," she said.

"But you," Mom said, "will always be my first baby. Even when you're grown up and graduated from college."

"I think I should graduate," Hanna said. "But we'll have to figure out what I'm graduating from."

"And what you're graduating to," Mom said. "Where you're going is even more important than where you've been."

The next day during David's nap, Hanna and her mom spread out the portfolio they'd been adding to since last summer. It was overstuffed, and Mom wanted to organize it.

Hanna enjoyed looking at everything she'd done. The least interesting thing was her "nines" homework. She told her mom they could recycle it. Her favorite thing was a photo of her life cycle drawing, which was way too big to put into the portfolio. It was hanging in her room.

There was also a photo of her "hydrangea" page, which had made Mom laugh so hard. Hanna still didn't see what was funny about hydrangeas, but she thought it was a nice drawing.

"You've done so much this year!" Mom said. "And look how your handwriting has changed."

The first paper in the portfolio was a letter Hanna had written to Gram in huge letters.

"I write smaller now," Hanna agreed. "And

neater."

"And your nines are the right way around," Mom said with a smile.

She held up a page of math problems Hanna had made up.

"I am so amazed at you, Hanna-bug," Mom said.

Hanna didn't know what the big deal was, but she didn't squirm when her teary-eyed mom gave her a big, wet kiss on the cheek.

chapter 13

The week that Dad was taking his final exams, Mom and Hanna called Carole and Henry in the mountains and they decided that everybody should graduate:

David was going to graduate from being a baby. He was going to be a big boy now and learn to pee in the toilet (or so Mom hoped).

Henry was going to graduate to Master Helper and be allowed to bring the garbage out at night, except when the bears might be cranky.

Dad was graduating from the school he was in, which was preparing him to be a nurse. Now he'd apply with his shiny good grades and year of experience in the hospital to a full nursing program, where he could get trained for a good job. "Maybe it'll be a job back in the mountains," Dad said with a wink.

Mom was going to graduate from "nervous homeschooling beginner" to "homeschooler." Mom explained that she was learning just like Hanna was, only a little bit more slowly!

Carole was going to graduate from working at a store to professional candle maker. She had been making candles for many years for her friends, and she was getting ready to sell her first ones in the store this coming Christmas.

Don was going to graduate from the long carpentry job he was finishing to a more relaxed summer.

Hanna had taken a very long time to figure out what she would graduate from and what she wanted to graduate to. Mom said what you were graduating *to* was even more important, but Hanna felt like they were two sides of the same thing.

First she thought she might graduate from mountain person to valley person, but she thought that like Dad, her heart had stayed in the mountains.

Then she thought she might graduate from a girl who couldn't do monkey bars to a girl who could, but she'd never quite made it all the way across. And also, when she thought about monkey bars it still made her mad that Kira had made fun of her.

She thought she might graduate from whatever grade she was in to the next one, but she and Mom decided that there wasn't one grade to describe her.

Finally, Hanna thought up her graduation all of a sudden one morning three days before they left for the mountains. She jumped out of bed and ran downstairs to the big roll of paper. She hauled it out and rolled some out on the floor. She lay down on it, then realized that there was a problem. She couldn't do the tracing herself!

"Oh, bother," as Winnie-the-Pooh would say.

Just then Gram came in and Hanna explained her problem.

"I need two outlines of myself," she said. "But I can't do my whole body. I can do my legs, but I have to sit up and then I can't do the rest of my body!"

Hanna was afraid that Gram might get cranky about this, because sometimes Gram thought Hanna's ideas were very silly and that Hanna asked for too much attention.

But this morning Gram seemed to be in a bit of a silly mood, herself, so she told Hanna to wait.

She went to her room and came back with the cane she used when the arthritis in her knees was hurting her a lot. She got a roll of tape from the sideboard, and a pencil.

"I'll hold the pencil against the cane," she said to Hanna. "You tape."

Hanna got what Gram was doing right away. She was making a very long pencil! Hanna taped the pencil securely to the cane then sat down again.

"I'm afraid the lines are going to be very shaky indeed," Gram said.

"That's OK," Hanna said. "I'm going to do it all over in marker."

So Gram draw a wobbly outline of Hanna on one paper, all the while grumbling about her shaky hands. But when Hanna stood up, they both giggled at the wobbly, flat girl on the paper.

Then Hanna rolled out more paper and Gram traced her again.

"Two shaky girls!" Gram said when they lined them up next to each other. "What are you going to do with that?"

"You'll see," Hanna said seriously. It was a big project. She was going to need oatmeal.

Gram and Hanna made oatmeal for themselves

and then for Mom and David. Hanna got dressed and brushed her teeth, and helped Mom unload the dishwasher. She was pleased that Mom called her "my big helper."

Then she got back to work.

On the first paper, she traced the shaky pencil lines about an inch too small, so that the girl who came out on the paper was smaller than Hanna. She gave the girl her own brown hair, but not so long, and her own blue eyes, but with no twinkles in them. The mouth was straight and serious. The girl wore Hanna's favorite dress from last summer, which was too small now, and shoes.

On the second paper, Hanna traced Gram's outlines at the same size, so she made a life-sized Hanna. Again she gave this Hanna her brown hair, but long enough for a ponytail like it was now. And she gave her blue eyes, with little silver twinkles from the glitter pen that she saved for very special art projects. She gave this Hanna toes and no shoes, and then made brown smudges on her knees and elbows and dripped colored paint on her hands.

As a last touch, she put a hand inside this Hanna's hand which led off the paper to another child, who was somewhere else.

After showing Gram her work, Hanna rolled up both pictures and tied them with string.

"These are to take to the graduation ceremony," she told Mom.

Hanna and her mom worked hard on graduation gifts, homemade for each person.

Gram bought a big flat of strawberries from a man who sold them on the corner, and she had Mom and Hanna help her make strawberry jam. She called it "sunshine in a jar," and she had Hanna write "J A M" on lots of little white labels that had flowers around the edges.

Mom told Hanna that Gram was famous for her jams when Mom was a girl.

Gram told Hanna that Mom never wanted to help when she was little, but she never had any trouble helping when it came to eating!

Mom stuck her tongue out at Gram and said that if Hanna believed everything Gram said, Hanna wasn't going to respect her mom very much anymore.

She and Gram laughed like that was the funniest joke ever.

This time the drive up to Carole and Don's was easy. Dad whistled tunes for Hanna to guess. They stopped in a park to have sandwiches.

Mom was singing songs with David and he was echoing the last word of each line.

"Old MacDonald had a farm, E-I-E-I-O," she sang.

"Oh!" David responded.

"The itsy bitsy spider went up the water spout."

"Thpout!"

Then Mom put a cassette of history stories that Karma had lent them into the car's cassette deck, and it hissed and crackled as it played a story about the Old West, which was what they were studying in history class now.

David went to sleep, and after a while, so did Hanna.

*

Carole and Don's cabin was very full this time because their neighbors didn't need house sitters. Mom and Dad and David slept on futons rolled out in the living room where the Christmas tree had been, and Hanna slept in Henry's bed, her head on the opposite end from his.

Dad went with Don on his job because Don needed help and was going to pay Dad. Dad said it would feel good to be making money the good, old-fashioned way and planted a kiss on Hanna's cheek when the sun was just coming up over the mountain.

There was a lot to be done. It was graduation day!

The graduation ceremony happened after dinner. Mom had made challah and Carole had made special candles to burn.

They left all the dishes for later, and Carole went around the whole living room lighting candles.

It was magical!

The pine scent of the mountain forests came in through the door, and Hanna could still feel the chill of the patches of snow that lingered on the hillsides.

The candles occasionally crackled, but everyone was quiet, even David.

Each person stood up in the middle of the circle and said what he or she had graduated from and to. Each family had made presents and handed them out:

David got a turtle with wheels that Don had made. When he pulled it, the turtle's shell went up and down. He also got a ceramic cup that Hanna had made in art class.

Henry got a new pair of pants his mom sewed, a big hammer from his dad, and another cup that Hanna made at art class (the better one, she thought, because David couldn't tell the difference!).

Dad got a nice new stethoscope that Gram had sent, a "best Daddy nurse" certificate that Hanna made, a knitted sweater Mom meant to have done for Christmas, and a bottle of fancy beer from Don.

Mom got a homeschooling book from Carole, a gift certificate from Dad that said he and Mom could spend a whole afternoon alone, without the kids (Hanna didn't really like that gift!), and a "best Mom teacher" certificate from Hanna, with a signature that David scribbled on it, too.

Carole got a framed picture of Hanna's whole family, including Gram, in front of the fanciest bride tree, a little fairy figurine from Don, and a necklace of beads that Hanna had made from clay

and string. She also got a teary hug from Mom, and Hanna wondered what there was to cry about!

Don got a coffee mug from Hanna, an old book that Dad had found at the library used book sale, a wax figurine from Carole to hang in his car, and a poem from Henry.

Hanna stood up and suddenly felt like she was going to cry, too. "This is better than Christmas and Chanukah," she said.

She unrolled her first picture, and showed herself as she was when they had moved to Gram's one year ago. At the top of the picture she had written H A N N A with the N's backwards, just like she made them then.

Then she unrolled the other picture. On top it said H A N N A, and the N's were all right because now they wanted to be.

On the bottom, with Gram's spelling help, Hanna had written:

H O M E S C H O O L E R

As it unfurled, she heard Carole say "Yes!" and Mom just say, "Ah."

"I graduated," Hanna said.

The stars twinkled in the windows. The candles hissed and crackled. It was the most beautiful night of the year.

About the Author

Suki Wessling has two children who have educated themselves both in school and in homeschool. Suki does pretty much every kind of writing you can do, including novels for kids and adults, articles for kids and adults, poetry, songs, and doodles. She wrote a homeschooling book for adults called *From School to Homeschool* (Great Potential Press). She blogs for adults at The Babblery (blog. sukiwessling.com) and for kids at KidsLearn (kidblog. sukiwessling.com). When she's not writing or teaching, she likes to play guitar and sing, cook, cuddle with cats, go on hikes, read, and hang out with family and friends.

Suki was inspired to write *Hanna, Homeschooler* when her homeschooling daughter complained that all chapter books seem to be about school.

Suki would like to thank everyone who helped her write, edit, and publish *Hanna, Homeschooler*, especially Abe and Charlotte, her homeschoolers, and Herb, husband and master copy editor.